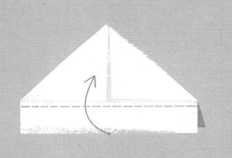

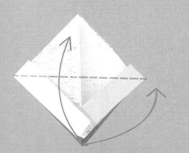

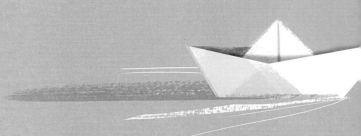

For my big brother

SIMON & SCHUSTER BOOKS FOR YOUNG READERS · An imprint of Simon & Schuster Children's Publishing Division · 1230 Avenue of the Americas, New York, New York 10020 · Copyright © 2015 by Daniel Miyares · All rights reserved, including the right of reproduction in whole or in part in any form. · SIMON & SCHUSTER BOOKS FOR YOUNG READERS is a trademark of Simon & Schuster, Inc. · For information about special discounts for bulk purchases, please contact Simon & Schuster Special Sales at 1-866-506-1949 or business@simonandschuster.com. · The Simon & Schuster Speakers Bureau can bring authors to your live event. For more information or to book an event, contact the Simon & Schuster Speakers Bureau at 1-866-248-3049 or visit our website at www.simonspeakers.com. · Book design by Chloë Foglia · The illustrations for this book are rendered digitally. · Manufactured in China · 0315 SCP

10 9 8 7 6 5 4 3 2 1

Library of Congress Cataloging-in-Publication Data · Miyares, Daniel, author, illustrator. · Float / Daniel Miyares. — First edition. · pages cm · Summary: "Wordless picture book about a boy who loses his paper boat in the rain"—Provided by publisher. · ISBN 978-1-4814-1524-8 (hardcover) — ISBN 978-1-4814-1525-5 (eBook) [1. Boats and boating—Fiction. 2. Toys—Fiction. 3. Lost and found possessions—Fiction. 4. Rain and rainfall—Fiction. 5. Stories without words.] I. Title. · PZ7.M699577Flo 2014 · [E]—dc23 · 2014016404

Float

Daniel Miyares

Simon & Schuster Books for Young Readers
NEW YORK LONDON TORONTO SYDNEY NEW DELHI

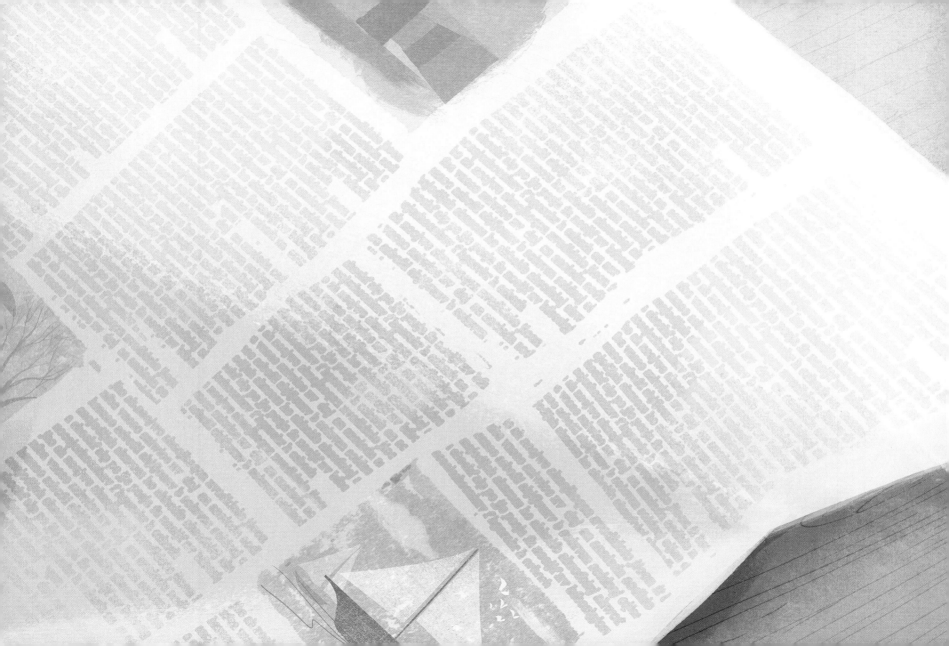

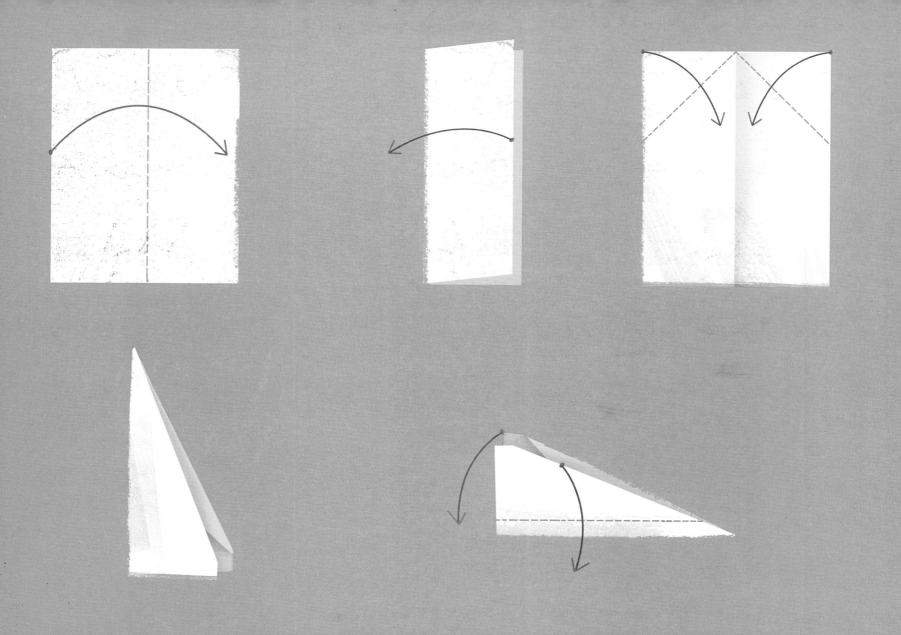